FIELD
NOTES

Memo Book
Durable Materials / Made in the UK

To Bronwen and David, bear spotters – M R.

For Sam Williams – D R.

Bloomsbury Publishing, London, Oxford, New York, New Delhi and Sydney

First published in Great Britain in 2016 by Bloomsbury Publishing Plc

50 Bedford Square, London WC1B 3DP

This paperback edition first published in 2017

www.bloomsbury.com

BLOOMSBURY is a registered trademark of Bloomsbury Publishing Plc

A CIP catalogue record of this book is available from the British Library

ISBN 978 1 4088 4555 4 (HB)   ISBN 978 1 4088 4556 1 (PB)
ISBN 978 1 4088 4557 8 (eBook)

All papers used by Bloomsbury Publishing are natural, recyclable products made
from wood grown in well managed forests. The manufacturing processes conform
to the environmental regulations of the country of origin.

Printed in China by C & C Offset Printing Co Ltd,
Shenzhen, Guangdong

1 3 5 7 9 10 8 6 4 2

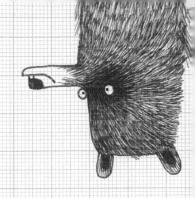

A Beginner's
Guide to
BEAR
SPOTTING

written by

Michelle
Robinson

illustrated by

David Roberts

BLOOMSBURY
LONDON OXFORD NEW YORK NEW DELHI SYDNEY

Going for a walk in BEAR country?

You'd better make sure you know your bears.

This is a **black** bear.

[Fig. 1. Black Bear, Ursus Americanus.]

This is a **brown** bear.

[FIG. 2. BROWN BEAR, URSUS HORIBILIS.]

And

that is . . .

. . . just plain SILLY.

I don't think you're taking this very seriously.
You ought to, you know.

Bears can be VERY dangerous.

If you get them muddled up, either one of them could **eat** you.

NOW are you paying attention?

Okay, here's what you need to know
before you start walking:

Black bears
are dangerous
and BLACK.

Brown bears
are dangerous
and BROWN.

Although sometimes **brown** bears can be a little BLACK . . .

. . . and **black** bears can be a little BROWN.

Don't worry.
Chances are you won't
even SEE a bear.

Oh, you LUCKY thing!

I think it's a **black** one.

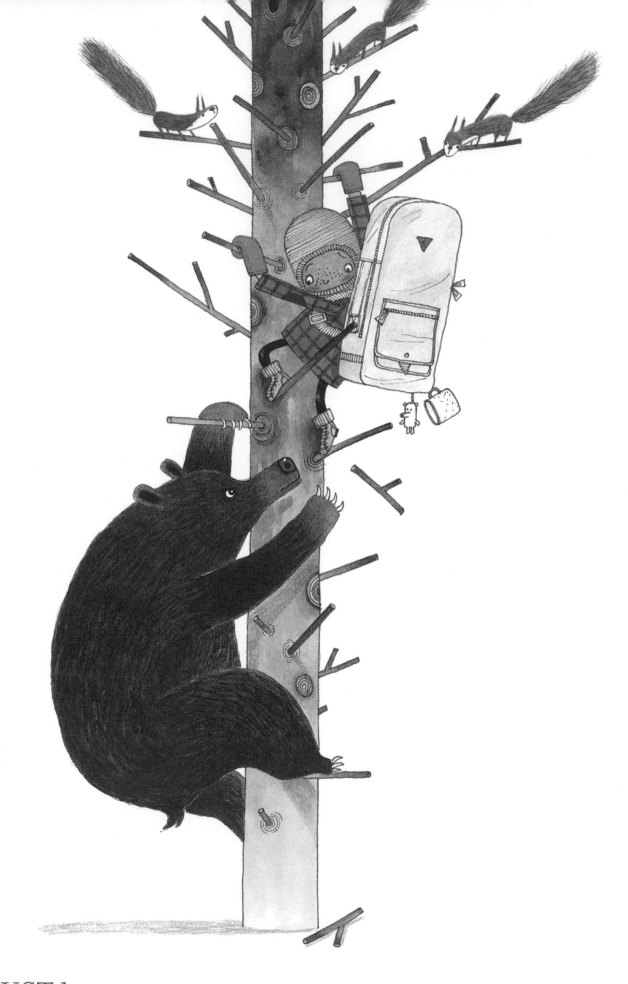

It MUST be.

Brown ones CAN'T climb trees.

Did you know **black** bears weigh around 400lbs?

With a **black** bear, the

best thing to do is back away *s l o w l y.*

This must be your LUCKY DAY.

You've found a **brown** bear too!

With a **brown** bear, the best thing to do is **play dead**.

Although to a **black** bear, that's like an invitation to dinner.

This would be a good time to use your pepper spray.

Pepper spray works on BOTH kinds of bears.

It makes them
d i z z y.

Or was it hungry?

Got any porridge?

GUM?!

What on earth are you going to do
with a pack of **gum**?

Of course.
Why didn't I think of that?

Quick!
Run for it!

Oops!

Well, I'm afraid I'm all out of ideas.
Got anything *else* in that bag?

Nope.

Too FLASHY.

That'll
NEVER do.

What did I tell you about
that silly thing?

It's soft and it's silly and it's . . .

. . . WONDERFUL!

It's working!

Well I never. I take it all back!

Bears *can* be dangerous . . .

. . . but they can also be
very, *very* sweet.

Psst!

Don't forget the golden rule
of BEARSPOTTING:

Real bears aren't this friendly,
you should only EVER snuggle up to the **stuffed** kind.

Don't say I didn't warn you.